Kailey And The Kittens

by

Shannon Hendel Belcourt

Twelve-year-old Kailey Kendall kicked the autumn leaves down the sidewalk on her way home from school. The cold wind whipped through her jacket, and her hands felt like ice.

On the street where she lived stood a shabby gray house, nearly blocked by massive trees that whispered secrets to anyone who dared come close enough. As she snuck through the damp uncut grass like a thief, the squawk of a magpie reminded her that she was an intruder.

Peeking through the window into a dimly lit dining room, Kailey saw the kittens in a cardboard box on the rug, where they had been since birth. Their mewing held her in a trance, until a twig cracked and an old woman appeared.

"You startled me," the woman said. "I was looking for my calico cat. I don't suppose you've

seen her?"

No," Kailey mumbled. "I came to see the kittens."

"Well, why don't you come inside where it's warm, and you can have a closer look."

Kailey wiped slick palms on her jeans, and went up the rickety steps.

"I'm Kailey," she said, shivering.

"I'm Mrs. Wakely," the old woman said, smiling. She hung up her sweater and Kailey's coat. "Would you like to stay for tea?" she asked.

Kailey answered, "Yes, please."

The apple-green kitchen smelled wonderful, like cinnamon and nutmeg, and when they went through to the dining room, Kailey noticed freshly cut flowers on the table. The kittens crawled on top of each other inside their box, and as Kailey knelt down, she could see they were all different colours.

Encouraged by Mrs. Wakely, she reached into the box and nuzzled each kitten, one by one. Kailey was in love!

"I've always wanted a kitten," the girl said wistfully.

Mrs. Wakely said, "Well, maybe you can have one of these."

"I've asked my parents before but they always come up with a reason to say no."

In the living room where Mrs. Wakely served the tea, Kailey spied several full grown cats lounging on the old furniture, peeking at her sleepily. There were knick-knacks in every little nook, giving it a sense of clutter, and yet it was tidier than at her house. Apart from a grandfather clock ticking in the corner, the only thing breaking the silence were the kittens, whining in their box.

"They haven't eaten since this morning," the old woman said. "I'm concerned about Misty, their mother. It's not like her to be away so long."

Kailey took her first sip of chamomile tea and bit into a homemade gingersnap cookie.

"Mmmm. Delicious," she said. The woman smiled, pleased. Kailey petted the older cats, asking their names. "Josie...Saffron...Pearl... Hobo...Amber...and Dazzle," she repeated, positive she would remember every one.

The whole time Kailey was there, she was trying to think of possible solutions to Mrs. Wakely's feeding problem and didn't realize how much time had passed until Mrs. Wakely closed the curtains.

Jumping up, the girl said, "I have to get home now. It's almost supper time."

Mrs. Wakely said kindly, "I'm so glad I met you, dear."

As she put on her coat and shoes to leave, an idea flashed through Kailey's mind, exciting her.

"Mrs. Wakely, if it's okay to come back after supper, I've thought of something we can try."

"Of course dear," she said, "if your parents don't mind."

Kailey knew that once the chores had been done, she would be free to do what she wanted. It was Friday night, her favorite night of the week. She rushed down the street to her home, bolting through the gate and up the front steps, into the house and kitchen.

"We were wondering where you were," Mom said, as she took the baked chicken from the oven.

"Sorry Mom." Kailey said. "I'll tell you about it at supper."

She washed up and helped her older

sister Kerry get the salad and vegetables ready. Younger sisters Holly and Hannah, aged eight and six, set the table, while Dad got the boys washed and seated.

"Are you up for some 'Hide 'n' Seek' later," he asked, "once these two are in bed?"

Dad had long ago started a 'game night' tradition on Friday nights, and Kailey regretted having to miss it.

"Sorry Dad. I'll be somewhere else after supper."

"Aw, too bad," he said.

Kailey had no appetite tonight, picking at her plate. Kerry rambled on about a boy at school, and everyone else had to wait to tell their stories of the day. As Kailey twitched in her chair impatiently, Dad started to chuckle.

"Go ahead, Kailey. Tell us what's making you so fidgety."

"But Dad," Kerry said, glaring at her sister, "I'm not finished talking."

"You are now," he said.

"There's this house on the corner," Kailey said. "An old woman named Mrs. Wakely lives there, and she has all these cats and five brand new kittens."

"I know her," Mom said. "I helped carry her groceries in from the car the other day."

Kailey's eyes lit up as she talked about the kittens, and while she had the attention of her whole family, she sucked in her breath and made a request.

"I was thinking that now might be the perfect time for me to have a kitten."

Kerry smirked, "Oh, really."

Kailey ignored her. Dad was already shoveling in his second helping of supper and Mom was busy with the twins, who mumbled in toddler-talk, so neither one replied right away.

The younger girls said, "We want a kitten."

Finally, Mom said, "Kailey, we've been through this before. We've got a full house and there's so much going on all the time. Looking after a pet is a lot of responsibility."

"But Mom! I'm very responsible. I do all my chores and sometimes Kerry's....and...and... my homework is always done right away, *plus* when she's not here, I babysit. You forget I'm almost thirteen."

"It's true, Mom. She helps me out a lot," Kerry said.

"We'll discuss it later," Mom replied.

"And we haven't forgotten how old you are," Dad said with a wink.

"It's not fair," Kailey said, annoyed at her parents. "I hardly ever ask you for anything." It was true - the last thing she had asked them for was a blue bike when she was ten. She excused herself from the table and began to clean up the dishes, her face sullen.

Dad headed to the den to play with the

younger kids and Mom went downstairs to fold laundry, while Kailey did the dishes and tidied the kitchen hurriedly. Kerry sauntered in briefly to help, but Kailey was glum.

"Kailey, remember how they were when I wanted to go out on my first date? It will be easier for you, 'cause I was the guinea pig."

"But don't you see? No matter what you do, I'm here to cover you. When do I get some independence?"

Kerry's date honked from the street, so she grabbed her purse and ran.

"We can talk later," she said.

Kailey went to the hall closet and scrounged through the various sizes of baby bottles, taking the ones with the smallest nipples, and shoving them into an old soccer bag. As a last

thought, she packed in a couple of her old stuffed animals as well.

Returning to the kitchen, she grabbed
a quart of goat's milk from the fridge just as
Mom came in for her evening cup of tea, book
in hand. Even though Kailey was still mad, she
could see how tired her mother was and felt a
tweak of sympathy.

"I hope it's alright if I take some milk,
Mom. Can you take it out of my allowance? It's
for the kittens."

Mom put the kettle on the stove to boil and
put ginger-lemon tea bags in the teapot.

"Of course you can," she replied, yawning.

"I'm going to Mrs. Wakely's now. The
kitchen's all clean."

"Okay. Make sure you wear your jacket,

honey."

As Kailey put on her mitts, she sighed.

"Mom, I'm not a little girl anymore."

It was dark and windy, and the air was heavy with the promise of snow. She hurried to Mrs. Wakely's house but had to wait a few minutes for the old woman to open the door.

"Hello, dear. I was trying to feed the kittens just now with an old eye-dropper, and I made a big mess of it."

Kailey grinned, unpacking the supplies from the soccer bag and handing them to Mrs. Wakely.

"When my baby brothers were born, my parents were worried because their tummies were always upset. My Mom hardly slept, and Dad felt bad 'cause he had to go to work, so

Auntie Bonnie came to stay with us to help out. Finally the doctors told my parents the babies were lactose-intolerant, and to replace regular cow's milk with goat's milk. After that, things got a lot easier around my house. So, I thought maybe the goat's milk would be good for the kittens."

Mrs. Wakely sterilized the bottles and heated up the milk. Then she and Kailey filled the bottles and began to feed the wriggling kittens. Once the little ones realized what was happening, they sucked down as much as their little tummies could manage, becoming very sleepy. Their heads drooped and when put back in the box, they purred as one. Kailey's stuffed animals took their mother's place, and the blanket was heated to warm them throughout

the night.

Mrs. Wakely was visibly relieved. "What a good idea you had, Kailey! I'm so glad your method worked."

It made Kailey feel good to see her smile.

They had tea while Mrs. Wakely asked Kailey about her family, and a couple of hours flew by. When the grandfather clock chimed eleven p.m., Kailey knew it was time to get home.

"I thought maybe I would go look for Misty tomorrow, with my friend Liz," Kailey said.

"Okay dear, but I'm hoping Misty will be back by morning."

"Well, I'll come anyway, Mrs. Wakely, just in case she isn't."

They said goodnight to each other and Kailey once more ventured out into the cold air. By the time she got home, her younger siblings were in bed and Mom and Dad were watching T.V. in the den.

Kailey went to her room, where she was surrounded by the things she loved: shelves with books, dolls, childhood toys and various art projects. The carpet and matching walls were blue, and covered in pictures of butterflies and kittens.

She heard Kerry come in the front door at midnight, trying to be quiet as she climbed the creaky stairs to her room next door. Kailey shut off the lamp and snuggled into the warmth of her quilt, thinking how nice it would be with a kitten to cuddle.

Early the next morning, Kailey took her best friend Lizzie over to meet her new friend, where they were told that the cat had not come home. After Mrs. Wakely served the girls tea and muffins, they hopped on their bikes, and set out to look for Misty.

"We're being detectives, Kailey," Lizzie

said. "Like Sherlock Holmes and Dr. Watson."

"Or Girl sleuths, like Nancy Drew and her friends."

They searched the neighbourhood for at least an hour, and then went to Lizzie's house to finish getting their Halloween costumes ready for that night. After lunch the girls headed out on their bikes again and crossed paths with a couple of boys they knew.

The one named Ronny inquired, "What were you doin' at that old witches' house this morning?"

"She's not a witch, you moron," said Lizzie.

"The little kids won't go to her house on Halloween!"

"It's true," said the other boy, Charlie. "Maybe Ronny's right."

"No, Charlie, he's not right. She wouldn't hurt anyone, and if you knew her, you would see what a nice lady she is."

"And she makes the best muffins!" Lizzie said.

"Well, we're just telling you the facts, Kailey, that's all."

Kailey was tempted to tell him where he could stick his facts, but since her thirteenth birthday was coming up soon, she decided to be mature and ignore him.

The girls decided to continue their search at the park, and the boys followed on their bikes. It was a huge park, with all kinds of play equipment. There were lots of trees and a picnic area, as well as many paths for hiking and bike riding. Without being asked, Ronny and Charlie helped them look for Misty. Although the kids saw several cats on their mission to find the missing feline, they finally had to give up and go home.

Kailey admitted to Lizzie, "I guess those

boys aren't so bad," and then she stopped in to update Mrs. Wakely.

"There are lots of cats at the park, Mrs. Wakely. Do you think they're all homeless?"

"I suppose some just wander," she replied. "It's in a cat's nature to do so, but most of them are good at finding their way, as mine always have."

When Kailey got home that day, she had a lot on her mind: Mrs. Wakely's worry about Misty, hungry kittens, and homeless cats. She made wieners and beans for supper but no one was very hungry.

The little kids especially were excited to go out Trick-or-Treating, door to door with Dad. Kerry was going to a party and was dressed like a hippie from the 60's. Mom took a picture of everyone all together, to add to the albums she had organized through the years.

As Dad left with two dragons, a puppy and a tiger, he said to Kailey and Lizzie, "Be careful out there, you two."

The Kids - Halloween

Kailey huffed, "Oh Dad, we're practically too old for this."

Dad grinned. "I guess you're right."

Dressed like Cinderella and Prince Charming, they met up with friends and ran from house to house, shrieking 'trick or treat!' Many families had taken the time to decorate their homes and porches with bats, cobwebs, pumpkins and witches, some even placing gravestones in the yards. Halloween was such a fun time for the kids, although a bit scary for the little ones. Kailey noted to Lizzie that a lot of grown-ups seem to really like it too.

Throughout the evening, all kinds of unusual creatures darted across their path, moving swiftly and loudly. No one cared how cold it was, and long after the small children had gone indoors, the older kids wandered the streets. When the porch lights had gone out in in the whole neighbourhood, the girls passed the run-down Wakely place on their way home, and Kailey understood at last why children avoided it altogether. It did look like one of those spooky houses from an old movie.

"I know what you're thinking, Kailey," Lizzie said. "It looks creepy, but only because it's not taken care of very well."

"I know, Liz. So let's change its reputation."

That night, while drinking hot cocoa that Kailey's Mom had made for everyone, the girls planned how they could get some outdoor chores done over at Mrs. Wakely's place.

The next morning, which was bright and

sunny in spite of the chill in the air, Kailey and Lizzie borrowed some tools from their parents and rounded up a bunch of friends from the neighbourhood.

They headed over to Mrs. Wakely's house, which looked a lot less threatening in the daylight. Under Kailey's guidance, they were there to work. She organized everyone into chores, which included mowing the lawn, trimming the hedges, weeding the garden, and removing many years of debris and trash.

There was plenty of work to get them through the afternoon, which resulted in a tidy and attractive yard. No longer hidden from view were late autumn asters and daisies surrounded by wildflowers.

"Now gang," Kailey said as Mrs. Wakely

served chocolate chip cookies and ice-cold milk to the workers. "The yard looks great and we've done a terrific job. But we still need to fix and paint the fence, and the garage will need some major work. How about if we all ask our parents for spare materials that we can use here? I know my dad has lots of paint in our garage. Let's see if we can do this before it gets too cold."

"I'm in," said Charlie, and the others agreed.

"Aw, thanks, everyone."

Mrs. Wakely said thank you to each of Kailey's friends individually and sent cookies home with them all.

"Lizzie," Kailey said later, "don't you think Mrs. Wakely looks better today?"

"Yup. She seemed really happy."

Since the first heavy snow fell three days later, most of their good intentions could not be fulfilled until spring. Still, the kids vowed to take turns shoveling Mrs. Wakely's snow and chipping the ice on the sidewalks. Kailey and Lizzie were already doing everyday tasks for her, and helping with the kittens, of course.

After a few weeks and a lot of care, the kittens were eating on their own. They climbed out of their box and explored the living room, chasing each other fast enough to smack into whatever was in their way. The girls and Mrs. Wakely chuckled constantly at the vigorous antics of the youngsters, while the older cats watched with disdain. Misty did not come home, and that made the old woman sad.

"My son gave her to me about a year ago,

after he found her underneath his car in the dead of winter. Until she went missing, I didn't worry about them, but now Hobo is the only one left to go outside."

"Someday," Kailey said, sharing one of her ideas with Mrs. Wakely as she often did, "I'm going to be a veterinarian, and hire people to help me find homes for all of the animals."

"You have a kind heart, my dear, and I am sure you will accomplish everything you set your mind to. I thought it was wonderful the way you organized your friends into helping me, without acting like a dictator."

Kailey was unaccustomed to the praise, but she liked it.

One evening a couple of weeks before Christmas, they were having their usual tea with cookies and Mrs. Wakely mentioned that it would soon be time to find homes for the kittens.

"Mrs. Wakely, would you mind if Lizzie and I, and some of our friends, put up notices all over the neighbourhood, asking if anyone wants to take one?"

"Well, you can try, dear," she said. "I really want them to go to loving homes. My son thinks that taking care of all of the cats is too much work for me now that I'm getting on in years, but he doesn't realize that they give me a purpose. And, if one needed a home, of course I wouldn't hesitate."

The following Saturday morning, which was particularly cold, Kailey, Lizzie, Ronny and Charlie posted ads on the doors of some of the

local businesses, like Mr. and Mrs. Morcini at

the grocery store, Dr. Connor's Veterinary, Mr.

Jonsson the dentist and Mr. Soon at the drug

store. When Kailey's Dad posted one at his job,

the other kids' parents did the same.

- KITTENS -

TO GIVE AWAY TO GOOD HOMES

ONE CALICO FEMALE

ONE BLACK FEMALE

ONE WHITE MALE

ONE ORANGE AND WHITE MALE

ONE BLACK AND WHITE FEMALE

By the day before Christmas, three of the five were already spoken for. The girls spent the afternoon of Christmas Eve at Mrs. Wakely's house, decorating. The ornaments were old, and hadn't been out of the box in years, so there was some gentle cleaning to be done.

Her son David had come with a little tree, which he set in the living room window, adding a string of lights. He was to pick her up the next day to come for Christmas dinner with his family, which included his wife and three boys.

"How come you don't see them more often?" Kailey asked Mrs. Wakely.

"Oh, they live in the big city, which is about three hours from here, and I can't drive my little car as far as that. David's job and family keep him busy, and my grandsons are very energetic."

"Kind of like my sisters and brothers, I suppose," Kailey said.

"And mine," said Lizzie, giggling. "I have eight brothers and sisters."

"That is a lot of children," said Mrs. Wakely. "I only have David."

That day, Mrs. Wakely had made sugar cookies, which she served with white cocoa and a cinnamon stick. "Thanks to you two, it looks festive in here for the first time in many years. I am most grateful, my dears."

Lizzie left early on Christmas Eve, since there were many things yet to do at her house before the next day, but Kailey stayed longer than usual, knowing it was to be her last time with three of the kittens. They would be picked up in the morning to go to their new homes for Christmas.

"I'm going to miss looking after them, Mrs. Wakely."

"Oh, I will too, Kailey. I'm a bit sad about it."

Kailey gave Mrs. Wakely a wrapped package.

"I hope you like it," she said. Her friend

opened it to find a picture frame, with a photo-

graph inside of the five kittens.

"I made the frame in shop class at school," Kailey said.

"I like it very much, dear. Thank you."

She gave Kailey a box of assorted homemade cookies, which were almost her favorite thing to eat.

Mrs. Wakely said, "Well, next time I see your mother, I'm going to tell her how well you have taken care of the kittens and that you arranged for your friends to come and work in the yard. Maybe my input will help them re-evaluate the situation."

"I think Dad would say yes this time if Mom said it was okay."

Mrs. Wakely appeared to think carefully before she answered. "It's hard to know what reasons people have for doing or not doing certain things, but your parents seem to have a great deal with which to be concerned."

Kailey shrugged. "I really try to see their

point of view, but sometimes I feel like they don't understand me at all."

"Well dear, no one wants to think about their children growing up."

But in the girl's heart, she wondered if that was the real reason.

She gave her friend a hug. "Thanks for everything, Mrs. Wakely. Merry Christmas."

"Merry Christmas, Kailey."

The Kendall family had gone out one evening to pick out a tree, and Dad had put the lights on, not even grumbling when they got tangled up. The four girls trimmed the tree, leaving the star on top for Dad, and extra care was taken with Mom's special ornaments. The kids cut snowflakes out of paper and coloured them brightly with crayons and sparkles, hanging them on the windows, while Dad put up the outside lights. It looked so pretty inside and out!

Kailey's family were happy to have Dad home for the holidays. On Christmas morning, they opened gifts in their pajamas and Mom made some specialty dishes for breakfast. Then Dad took all the kids to a local hill for sledding in the afternoon, where there were many families doing the same. What fun everyone had bombarding each other with snowballs!

When it was time to prepare dinner, each of the girls did her share, with Dad in charge of the turkey. Mom had baked pies and the meal was delicious. Then Kerry took care of all the clean-up.

"This time, you get the night off, Kailey. I owe you a lot of favours."

Kailey eagerly played games with Dad and the younger children while Mom relaxed in her rocking chair. When they were all ready to sit in the den to watch a Christmas movie, with treats and cocoa, Kailey had a new question to ask her parents.

"Would it be alright to have Mrs. Wakely come for dinner once a week? I think she needs to get out of her house sometimes, and she doesn't seem to have any friends."

"That's a nice idea, honey," her mother said.

"You and your friends have sure been helping her out ever since those kittens were born." Dad grinned. "Even Ronny is showing his good side."

"Her cookies are the best," Kerry said.

It had been a wonderful Christmas with the family and the next day, Kailey spent at Lizzie's house. Mrs. McKinney was always cheerful and the nine children, aged three to eighteen, would often conjure up new and terrific games to play.

Mr. McKinney, an inventor in his spare time, was constantly building something interesting, and this holiday it was a light-weight board on which they could slide down the huge hill in their backyard. No ski poles were required and they had a blast.

Kailey decided to stop in at Mrs. Wakely's house before supper, and was disappointed to find the old woman wasn't there. It was snowing heavily and the trees sparkled in white. Every house along the street was lit up for the holiday, making a glorious picture.

As she entered her home, the aroma of supper in the oven made her aware of how ravenous she was, and a surprise guest greeted her as she entered the kitchen.

"Hello dear," a cheery voice said.

"Hi honey," Mom said, smiling at her.

"Hi Mom. Mrs. Wakely, I got worried when you weren't home."

"Oh, your mom asked me for supper today. But I had to be careful on the sidewalk."

Kailey's Mom was apologetic. "I'll ask Joe to put sand on the ice."

"I can walk home with you after supper," the girl offered.

Her hands were freezing, and the cocoa Mom had made warmed her all the way through. She could hear Christmas music playing quietly on the small radio, and muffled laughter from the den where Dad was spending quality time with the other kids.

"Honey, Mrs. Wakely has told us so many good things about you, and your dad and I came to the conclusion that we've been a little unfair. We're very proud of the way you've handled all the extra responsibility."

But what does that mean, Kailey wondered? She heard a familiar noise coming from Mrs.

Wakely's large handbag, which had been hidden under the table. Out came the squirming black and white kitten, the one Kailey wanted most for her very own. Her heart leapt with joy!

"I know she's your favourite," the old woman said, holding her out to Kailey, who took the soft, warm kitten in her arms.

"It was Mrs. Wakely's idea to bring her today." Mom told her, with a broad smile.

"Oh, thank you!" Kailey's eyes brimmed over with happy tears. The best thing ever had just happened and she felt like her world was complete. "I'm going to call her Molly." Kissing her kitten on the nose, she asked her friend, "Can I still come over for tea?"

Mrs. Wakely smiled. "I wouldn't have it any other way."

THE END

Made in the USA
Charleston, SC
29 January 2016